Just My Style

by Diane Z. Shore and Jessica Alexander • illustrated by Kelly Canby

To my sister, Carol, who has her own unique style . . . back on! —D.Z.S.

For Kelly, my favorite everything. —J.A.

For my ever so stylish sister, Claire. —K.C.

Text copyright © 2018 Diane Z. Shore and Jessica Alexander.
Illustrations copyright © 2018 Kelly Canby.

Published in 2018 by Amicus Ink, an imprint of Amicus
P.O. Box 1329 • Mankato, MN 56002
www.amicuspublishing.us

Library of Congress Cataloging-in-Publication Data
Names: Shore, Diane ZuHone, author. | Alexander, Jessica, author. | Canby, Kelly, illustrator.
Title: Just my style / by Diane Z. Shore and Jessica Alexander ; illustrated by Kelly Canby.
Description: Mankato, Minnesota : Amicus Ink, [2018] | Summary: "On the way to the hair salon,
young Anna imagines herself in a myriad of different hairstyles—and life styles—until finally,
she decides that being herself is the best choice"—Provided by publisher.
Identifiers: LCCN 2017014778 | ISBN 9781681522029 (library bound : alk. paper)
Subjects: | CYAC: Haircutting—Fiction. | Individuality—Fiction.
Classification: LCC PZ8.3.S55918 Jus 2018 | DDC [E]—dc23
LC record available at https://lccn.loc.gov/2017014778

Editor: Rebecca Glaser
Designer: Kathleen Petelinsek

First Edition 9 8 7 6 5 4 3 2 1
Printed in China

Just My Style

by Diane Z. Shore and Jessica Alexander

illustrated by Kelly Canby

amicus ink

Mankato, Minnesota

I'm off to get a haircut,

A people-stop-and-stare cut,

A full-of-fun-and-flair cut . . .

Something very me.

Perhaps I'll get a mop cut,

A raggy, shaggy top cut,

A hide-inside-it lop cut . . . .

NO, that's just not me.

Maybe then a crew cut,

A stand-up-straight salute cut.

Obey-or-get-the-boot! cut . . . .

NO, that's hardly me.

Maybe then a poodle cut,
A curly, corkscrew noodle cut,

An ooh-la-la to you-dle cut . . .

No, that's SO not me.

I think I'll get a ponytail,
A swirls-like-macaroni tail,

To twirl while on the phone-y tail . . .

NO. That's my big sister.

Or bouncy, flouncy pigtails.
Some ribbons-tied-up-big tails,

Some dance-an-Irish-jig tails . . . .

Maybe . . .

Or else I'll get a page cut,
A movie-star-on-stage cut,

The one that's all the rage cut . . .

NO, that's not quite me.

I know!
I'll get a funky cut,
A way-up, way-out punky cut,

A purple, spiky, spunky cut . . .

NO, that's way not me.

NO!

Definitely not me!

Or maybe get a short cut,

A more outdoorsy-sport cut,

A slam-dunk, down-the-court cut . . .

That's sometimes me.

"Anna, you're next!"

Oh, it's my turn?

I'd like . . .

A little-off-the-ends cut,

My jump-rope-with-my-friends cut,

A leave-it-all-in-place cut,

My perfect-for-my-face cut.

The who-I-want-to-be cut,

The only-one-like-me cut . . .

YES!

That's ME!